Christian, Peggy.

The bookstore mouse.

DATE			

The
Bookstore
Mouse

Peggy Christian

Illustrated by

Gary A. Lippincott

JANE YOLEN BOOKS

HARCOURT BRACE & COMPANY

San Diego New York London

Library of Congress Cataloging-in-Publication Data
Christian, Peggy.
The bookstore mouse/by Peggy Christian;
illustrated by Gary A. Lippincott.—1st ed.
p. cm.
"Jane Yolen books."
Summary: A mouse living in an antiquarian bookstore learns the true power of words when he literally falls into a medieval tale and helps defeat the dragon Censor.
ISBN 0-15-200203-0
[1. Mice—Fiction. 2. Bookstores—Fiction.
3. Books and reading—Fiction. 4. Dragons—Fiction.]
I. Lippincott, Gary A., ill.
II. Title.
PZ7.C45284Bo 1995
[Fic]—dc20 95-8454

Designed by Camilla Filancia
The text type was set in Granjon.

G F E D

Printed in the United States of America

For my mother,

who opened the door to the magic in books

And Barbara Fox,

who taught me more of the magic

in her bookstore, where Cervantes lives

Contents

The Bookstore Mouse

PROLOGUE

Of Some Things That Relate to This Adventure

On the corner of Ninth and Market streets downtown, there is a bookstore. It is very different, though, from the bookstores you may know, because it is an antiquarian bookstore. In this bookstore there are no bright and colorful books filled with characters. Nor are there any books with pictures that pop up when you open them. There are no books with flaps to lift, or wheels to turn, or games to play.

In fact, if you look in the window of this bookstore, all you see are long rows of dusty old books. They are stacked in great leaning piles on the floor, crammed into the tall wooden shelves that reach from floor to ceiling, and scattered over every table and countertop. Just looking at them, you might think they are very dull books indeed. But a book cover can be very deceiving, especially books as old and faded as these.

At one time, looking in the window, you might have also noticed something else that made this bookstore different. In the corner, at the end of *The Complete Works of Bulwer-Lytton,* you might have glimpsed the tip of a furry tail. And if you had moved down and peered in carefully through the dingy glass you would have seen Milo, the bookstore cat. He would have been doing what any cat who can't read would be doing in a bookstore—sleeping.

Sleeping was not the only thing Milo did, however. He also guarded the books from mice. But there was one mouse that Milo could never catch. That mouse lived behind the books in the reference section. There, big fat volumes like dictionaries and encyclopedias and almanacs made a thick wall, impossible for Milo to get through. The only gap in the wall was where one volume leaned against the next. But the small, triangular opening was filled with a wad of paper.

Milo knew the mouse was back there though, because every once in a while it threw out scraps of paper, just to taunt him. Until one day—a day that changed everything for both of them.

CHAPTER I

Wherein Cervantes the Bookstore Mouse Recounts a Day Like Any Other—Almost

I REMEMBER WELL THE DAY IT HAPPENED. It started out just like any other day. I was safe and secure behind my wall of books in the reference section. I could hear the click, click, click of the cat's claws as it paced back and forth.

"After supper," I thought, "I must find a few **SHARP WORDS** to throw at him." But first, I needed to decide what to eat. There were lots of recipes to choose from, because I ate my meals out of a thick cookbook. Before it had fallen down from the cooking section, three shelves above, I was limited to the few **TASTY WORDS** I could find scattered in my dictionary. But with the cookbook, all I had to do was tear out the list of ingredients and mix the words together. Then I could enjoy such delicacies as *Mexican rice* or *Cajun chicken*.

That day I had had a hard time deciding what to eat. *Barbecued ribs?* No, they sounded a bit sticky. *Hawaiian pork chops?* Too exotic. I'd never come across *Hawaiian* before and I didn't want to take a chance. But then I found it. *Roast pork with herbs*. Anything with the word *herbs* in it was bound to be good; they added such flavor to a meal. After I had chosen my entree, I slowly carved the paper with my nail, careful to slice through only the top layer. If I cut too deep, I would lose the recipe on the back of the page. But the paper in this cookbook was thick and of good quality, and it was easy for me to peel off the words.

With all the ingredients assembled, I wadded them up and popped the succulent morsel into my mouth. I rolled the words around on my tongue . . . *rosemary, oregano, thyme, sage* . . . oh, they were so delicious!

When the last letter had been swallowed, I patted my stomach and went to relax on the open pages of the dictionary. Crawling into the crack at the center of the book, I snuggled down with my head on the word *siesta*.

Following a quick catnap (a nap to rest up for my battles with the cat) I started searching for a few HARSH WORDS to throw at the cat. After all, a mouse is only as good as his word.

Not far from *siesta* in my dictionary I found *remark*. I knew that if I folded it right, I could make a POINTED REMARK. In any argument it is important to get to the point as soon as you can.

Then I chose the word *fun*. Now that may seem like a strange choice at first, because it is so short. But I had often been told by my mother that poking *fun* at someone was a good way to hurt them. I wasn't sure I wanted to get close enough to the cat to poke him, but it might come in handy as a last resort.

The other word I chose was *zymurgy*. Its definition has to do with a branch of chemistry, but that wasn't why I chose it. I picked this one because it was the last word in my dictionary. Surely the best way to win an argument is by getting in the last word.

I gathered up my arsenal and crawled up the edge of volume A of the encyclopedia. I left the words up there so I could hurl them down at the cat the next time he came by.

But my work still wasn't done. I had to check the hole. You see, the wall of encyclopedias was good and solid—except for one little gap. That gap was caused by some human who had not carefully lined up the books on the shelf. The thirteenth volume of the encyclopedia was leaning against the fourteenth volume. It formed a triangular hole large enough for the cat to get its paw in, and I was always working to fill the hole.

I relied on my trusty dictionary and had built the foundation of my defense from the longest words I could find, words like *flocci-naucinihilipification* and *antidisestablishmen-tarianism*. I was always careful to choose good sturdy words that only have one or two meanings. I stayed away from loose, flabby words like *run,* which has over forty different definitions.

That day I added three impenetrable words, *pontificating, filibustering,* and *sesquipe-dalian*. I stuffed the new words into the hole and stood back to admire my work. My **WALL OF WORDS** was magnificent—absolutely invincible.

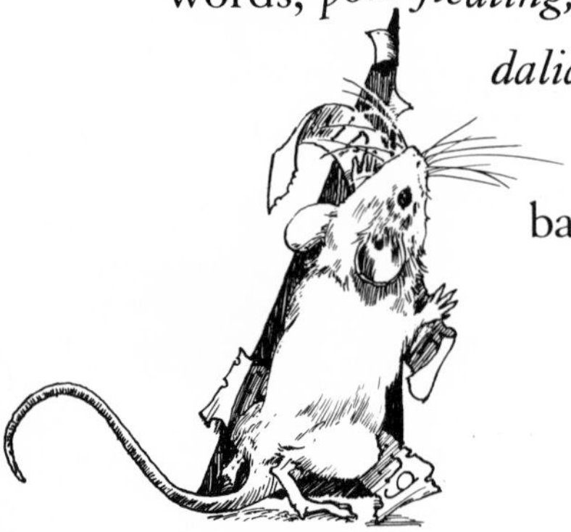

CHAPTER 2

A Further Account of That Almost Normal Day

NO SOONER HAD I DECIDED TO HEAD BACK TO MY cookbook for a little snack when I was startled by a terrible thudding noise. This was a menace worse than the cat. This was a human. It got closer and closer and I lay quivering in my dictionary, hoping that it would pass by. But it didn't. I heard a low rumbling sound and I could understand a bit of it—*let's see . . . old set . . . not too much out of date . . . try . . .*

And then the books started to shake, and a shaft of light flashed across the page where I was huddled. I scrunched my eyes up against the unaccustomed brightness. A beam of light poured in, dust sparkles dancing through it. I moved very slowly off the page, toward the wall of books that still remained standing. What could I do? The gap was large enough for a cat. Trying to think clearly about my predicament, I crouched trembling against a book.

And then the shaft of light dimmed and the edge of a book came bursting through the gap. Shaking from the top of my ears to the tip of my tail, I looked toward where the opening had been, but once again a solid wall rose to my right.

I leaned back in relief and listened as the human moved about on the other side of the books. The books began to shake again, and this time the book I was leaning on was pulled right out from under me. I toppled backward and tumbled off the edge of the shelf. I was falling. I'd had this same sensation in dreams, but now it was real and I seemed to be plummeting downward forever. Mere words, even for a word wizard like me, cannot describe the horror of that fall.

When I hit bottom I found myself on the top of the human's shoe. The human let out a piercing screech and then roared, "Ahhhhhh, a mouse!"

The human began to shake its shoe. I grabbed hold of the laces to prevent myself from being dashed against the bookcase. When the shoe came down on the floor again, I leaped off and scrabbled away as fast as I could—away from the shoes that came stamping after me, barely missing my tail. I made it to the edge of the bookcase and dove behind the books on the bottom shelf.

Finding myself in a passage clogged with dust balls, I sneezed as the dust I'd churned up tickled my nose. I strained to hear. The thud-shuffle of the shoes paused at the end of the bookcase and waited, and then, much to my relief, began to move away until all I could hear was the sound of my own heart pounding in my chest.

It was a very long time before I dared to move even a whisker. I was afraid the human would come back again and begin tearing down the book walls. I was afraid the cat would come and smell me out, and there I was, me of all mice, at a total loss for words. Finally, unable to stand the tension any longer, I began to slink deeper into the passage, looking for a safe place to hide.

I thought sadly of my wonderful haven now four shelves above me. I thought of the arsenal of words I had built up and of how in the end, my words had failed me. And then I thought of my cookbook and all the delicious morsels stored up there, and my stomach felt twisted and empty. I started to cry.

My tears made everything all blurry, and I didn't notice the book until I smashed my nose on it. It lay unopened on the shelf behind the other books. Even through the layer of dust on its cover, I could see that it was a beautiful book, bound in leather and heavily embossed in gold. Reaching up, I tried to lift the cover, but I wasn't quite tall enough. I dug the toes of my hind feet in between the pages and grasped the cover of the book. Slowly, using the rough edges of the pages as a ladder, I managed to push the cover higher and higher and higher until it stood upright. It wobbled for a moment, threatening to come down on my head, and finally fell open the other way.

Pushing back a few blank pages, I stopped at the first one with writing. *Perhaps,* I thought, *I'll be able to find some* **words of comfort**. But the words on that page were nearly as big as I was, and written with funny fat letters all woven together with curlicues and flourishes. I couldn't make out a one of them.

I pushed aside a few more pages until I came to one covered with regular words. At the top of the page stood bold letters spelling out Chapter One.

Below that I found the word *Far*. That wasn't much comfort at all. It just made me think of how far from home I was. I read the

next one, *away*. That was no better. I didn't want to be reminded I was away from home either. Next I read *and*. And . . . and . . . and what? That was my problem. And what would become of me? Moving down the line of words I found *long*. Long cat's teeth. Long cat's claws. That was what *long* made me think of. I moved on quickly. *Ago*—the past. The past when I had been safe and secure in my haven. This book wasn't helping at all.

I was starting to feel very sorry for myself. And the sorrier I felt, the more the words resounded in my mind. *Far . . . away . . . and . . . long . . . ago*. My home was far . . . far away. And it seemed long . . . long ago. As I brooded, the words strung themselves out in my brain and I saw that when they were said one after the other it meant something. They were not just a list of words, they were like someone talking in my mind. "Far away and long ago," they said.

I looked at the next few words and tried to follow along as they marched across the page. *Far away and long ago . . . was home,* I thought. But that's not what the voice said as I read the words. "Far away and long ago, in medieval England, there lived a young monk named Sigfried." And the words swept around me and through me and carried me away.

But the place where I found myself was not my haven. Instead it was a very foreign and strange-looking world.

CHAPTER 3

Of the Stupendous Adventure That Befell Cervantes in the Book

THE NEXT FEW SENTENCES TOOK ME DOWN a long, damp passageway. My tail dragged across broad, flat stones that seemed to be rubbed smooth by years of wear. Rock walls rose on either side, and in front of me stone stairs wound out of sight.

I looked all around and strained my ears, but there was no sign of the cat. I was pretty sure I wasn't in the bookstore any more, although I had no idea where else I could be. Very cautiously I crept along the passage-way until, quite suddenly, something loomed up in front of me. I stopped in my tracks and stared. It was a word, a very strange word that I had never seen before.

One by one I read the letters in the dim light:

I was really perplexed. I kept looking at the word until the rock walls dissolved around me and the rock floor disappeared from beneath my feet and to my amazement, I found myself back on the shelf in the bookstore, squatting on the open book.

The word was right under my nose. But how in the world was I going to find out what it meant? My dictionary was inaccessible four shelves up. I turned around and tried to make my way back to it, but somewhere off in the distance I heard the cat snarl, and I knew I couldn't chance it. I had to find a way around the word.

Diving back into the beginning of the story, I scurried along the passage until I came up against the strange word again. It seemed solid as the rock walls, but I plunged ahead and to my very great surprise, I managed to squeeze between the *p* and the *t*. In front of me, the passage continued, and I saw that I was much closer to the staircase. A shiver ran down my back at the sight. I had never skipped through a word I didn't know before, and I was surprised that there was anything on the other side.

Scuttling across the slippery floor toward the bottom of the staircase, I made my way deeper and deeper into the story. The scrabbling of my paws echoed in the stony silence, and I felt both terrified of what I might be getting into and frightfully curious. I had never been the sort to go headfirst into the unknown, and I could not believe my recklessness.

I reached the bottom step and peered up into the gloom. By standing on the tips of my hind paws, I could just reach the edge of the next step. Using my tail for an extra boost, I pulled myself up. Around and up, higher and higher I went, until I came to the top step, and the doorway of a small, dismal room.

Standing in that doorway, I suddenly felt very exposed, so I dashed over to the closest wall and began to nose around. The room smelled vaguely familiar. It was the same musty odor as the bookstore, only much stronger. I took a quick inventory of my surroundings. On the wall across the room, bookcases of large leather books rose to the ceiling.

But these books were quite different from the ones I knew at home. They were huge and brilliantly decorated, their covers shining with gold and jewels. There were only a few books on each shelf, and they were chained to the wall behind them.

I was overcome by their beauty, and I wanted to get closer and touch their glimmering jeweled covers. So intent was I, in fact, that I didn't watch where I was going. My whiskers brushed against something to my left and I froze. Very slowly I turned and found myself staring up the leg of a human.

Somehow, this human seemed very strange though. For one thing he was smaller than the ones I'd seen before. I decided he must be very young. For another thing he was dressed not in the long pants of most other humans but in some kind of robe.

Knowing how humans felt about mice, I knew my only chance was to escape into an opening too small for his hand. But I was not quick enough, and just as I had spotted a likely escape route, the human moved his foot and bumped me.

"Oh, odsplut!" he cried, bending over me. I tried to make a run for it, but quite suddenly I felt his hand wrap around my body, holding me just tightly enough to prevent my escape. He lifted me up and poked my nose down at an inky black spot on the paper.

"Look what you have made me do, you little . . . little, oh, whatchamacallit!" With his free hand he tried to clean up the mess with his sleeve. His efforts only made it worse, the ink smearing all over the page.

"Let me go," I said, squirming to get out of his grasp.

"What is this? Did you speak? No, of course not, it is only my imagination again," he said.

"It is not your imagination," I said, quite insulted. "Why shouldn't I speak, for heaven's sake! You do, don't you?"

"Me? Of course, but I am a person. I have always been able to talk. Ever since I can remember."

"Well, me, too," I said. "The part about talking, that is. Not the part about being a person. I'm a mouse."

"I can see that," he said. "Do you have a name?"

"My name is Cervantes."

"That is a very odd name. Spanish perhaps? I do not recall hearing it before. Mine is . . ."

"Yes, I know. It is Sigfried. I can read."

"Where did you come from?" he asked.

Now this was a bit of a stumper. I wasn't exactly sure how I had gotten into this strange place. I had been running from the cat, and then I'd found the book on the shelf, opened it, and then . . .

"I am not sure," I told him. "I just seem to have stumbled into your story and gotten all caught up in it."

"My story?"

"Yes, your life seems to be an open book."

"An open book? Yes, I suppose it is. At least I always seem to have one in front of me to copy," Sigfried said, picking up the ruined page and setting it on the floor next to him.

"Parchment is very . . . very . . . oh yes, expensive, you know, and that is the third leaf I have ruined this month. The armarius will be frightfully angry."

"Armarius?"

"Yes. He is the monk who oversees the scribes. That is what I am. Not an armarius, a scribe. I wanted to be a knight like my brother George, but I am a . . . a . . . a howd'yacallit . . . a younger son, so they sent me to this monastery. The . . . whosits put me to work here in the scriptorium."

There was that word again. Only this time I didn't have any trouble getting past it. In fact, I had the feeling that I knew what it might be.

"Anyway," Sigfried went on, "it wasn't the wisest choice because I do not seem to have a way with words."

You can say that again, I thought. I had never seen anyone stumble around so trying to find the right one.

"And now I must complete this page that I am working on," Sigfried said. "You may stay and watch if you like. It is nice to have the com . . . com . . . "

"Companionship?" I asked.

"Yes . . . and the help with words."

CHAPTER 4

Of the Discourse Between Cervantes and Sigfried and Other Matters Worth Relating

I FOUND A CORNER OF THE DESK WHERE I COULD sit and not be in Sigfried's way as he worked. Choosing another page of parchment, he spread it before him. He began by pricking holes with a sharp, pointed instrument down each side of the page.

"Oh, so that's an *awl,*" I said. "I saw it before, lying on your desk, but it was such a **SHARP WORD** and I was afraid of getting stuck on the point, so I skipped over it. Now that I see you using it, I understand what it is. It's like the word *parchment*. I didn't know what that was either until I saw you blot it."

"Please, do not remind me," Sigfried said. Setting the awl down, he took up a metal stylus and began to draw lines across the page, from hole to hole. Then he turned the page and drew lines lengthwise to mark what I guessed to be the margins. Setting those two instruments carefully aside, he took up his quill pen and dipped it into the ink. Very slowly and carefully he began to copy letters from the open book at his side.

Just then we heard heavy footsteps on the staircase beyond the door.

"Quickly!" Sigfried whispered. "Up my sleeve and into my hood. You must not be seen."

I ran up Sigfried's arm, the rough material providing a good grip for my claws. I had barely made the edge of the hood and jumped in, when I heard someone step into the room. A strange voice spoke.

"You have not finished your work even yet, Sigfried?"

"The work goes slowly, Brother."

"Too slowly. I feel your mind must be elsewhere. Have you been daydreaming again?"

"No, Brother. I mean, yes, Brother. Perhaps just a little." Sigfried bowed his head.

I peeked over the edge of Sigfried's hood at the stranger. *That must be the armarius,* I thought.

He pointed at the blotched parchment. "Another leaf ruined, I see." He looked at it more closely. "Not only are you careless, you are guilty of cacography."

"I am sorry, sir. I never mean to commit oh . . . whatayacallit? . . . I am afraid I have failed you again."

The armarius looked at the parchment that Sigfried was working on.

"Allow me to see the original you are working from," he said.

Sigfried leaned to the side and the armarius compared the original to Sigfried's copy.

"These are not the same words," he said.

"No? Let me see. No, I suppose they are not. But they mean the same thing," Sigfried said.

"Meaning should not concern you. A scribe must be careful and deliberate. Attend to the individual words, Sigfried. You must get the words correct. The meaning will take care of itself."

The armarius looked at him sadly. "You cannot seem to keep your mind on the task at hand. Our work requires complete concentration and dedication. You must accept your station in life, Sigfried, and make the most of what you are."

"I will try to do better, Brother."

"I am afraid you will have to stay here for the rest of the day to finish your work. The other scribes will spend the afternoon at a special Mass for the bishop. I am sorry, Sigfried, but your duty comes first."

"I understand, Brother," Sigfried said, and the armarius turned and left the room.

I stayed nestled in Sigfried's hood until the armarius's footsteps could no longer be heard in the hall. It was warm and cozy in there, and I was strongly tempted to take a short nap. After all, this way of reading—getting all caught up in a story—was very tiring. But somehow the words kept pushing me on, so that I couldn't stop. I scrabbled out of Sigfried's hood and down his sleeve to the tabletop.

"Cacography sounds like a very terrible charge," I said.

"Well, for a scribe, bad handwriting and poor spelling are real handi . . . handiwhatsises . . . oh yes, handicaps. Anyway, he is always upset with me for one thing or another. I just do not have a good command of words. But that is the life of my story. . . . I mean the story of my life."

I felt quite sorry for the chap. After all, I

was a true wizard with language, a regular lexicologist. Perhaps, with all my knowledge, there was some way I could give him a way with words. A gift of gab, so to speak. I was pondering the idea when we suddenly heard steps approaching in the hall.

"Someone else is coming!" Sigfried cried. "Hurry! Back into my hood."

I scurried up Sigfried's sleeve and dropped into his hood just as a loud knock sounded at the door. I balanced on a fold so I could see over the edge. Sigfried went to the door and opened it just a crack.

CHAPTER 5

A Strange Happening, Not More Strange Than True

A RAIN-SOAKED LAD STOOD AT THE DOOR, HOLDING a crumpled and muddy piece of parchment. "Is the armarius in?" he asked through chattering teeth.

"I am afraid all of the monks and the . . . the . . . well, the one you asked about . . . they are all at a special Mass for the bishop," Sigfried said.

"Would you give him this message as soon as he returns? I must get back to my hearth and dry off before I catch my death." The boy began to hand the parchment to Sigfried but then pulled back. "Can you be trusted?" he asked. "This is a very serious matter."

"Yes, of course," Sigfried assured him. "I will see that he gets it straight as an arrow . . . er, I mean, straightaway."

The boy looked as if he didn't trust Sigfried at all, but his desire for a warm fire and hot soup must have overcome his doubts, because he thrust the parchment into Sigfried's hands and hurried away.

Sigfried placed the message on his desk and returned to his work.

"Aren't you going to read it?" I asked.

"No, it is not for me, it is for the armarius."

I tried to settle in the folds of the hood and watch Sigfried's progress with his tedious work, but I couldn't contain my curiosity about the message.

"Perhaps you should take the message to the armarius right now," I suggested.

"And interrupt the bishop's Mass? I think not. He will return to check on my progress as soon as they are finished. And with all these interruptions, I will have nothing to show him. Now, please be quiet so that I might . . . might oh . . . howd'yacallit . . . oh yes, concentrate."

But I couldn't stand to see that parchment lying there unread. *Sigfried won't read it,* I thought, *but I see no reason why I couldn't have just a peek at it. What harm could that do?* So I crawled out of the folds of the hood and then down Sigfried's arm as carefully as I could, so as not to disturb him. Very quietly, I snuck a look at the message.

It was addressed to someone, but it was impossible to make out who. The parchment had gotten wet, and there were big black splotches where the ink had run.

"Sigfried," I called. "Sigfried, I think it

would be all right if you wanted to read this. The name of the person it is addressed to has been wiped out. Perhaps it was intended for you all along. You should at least come see."

"Cervantes, I will not read that message. The lad said very clearly that it was for the armarius. Now do be quiet!"

The boy could have been wrong, I thought to myself. Anyway, I did not have such fine scruples. I read on, past the salutations.

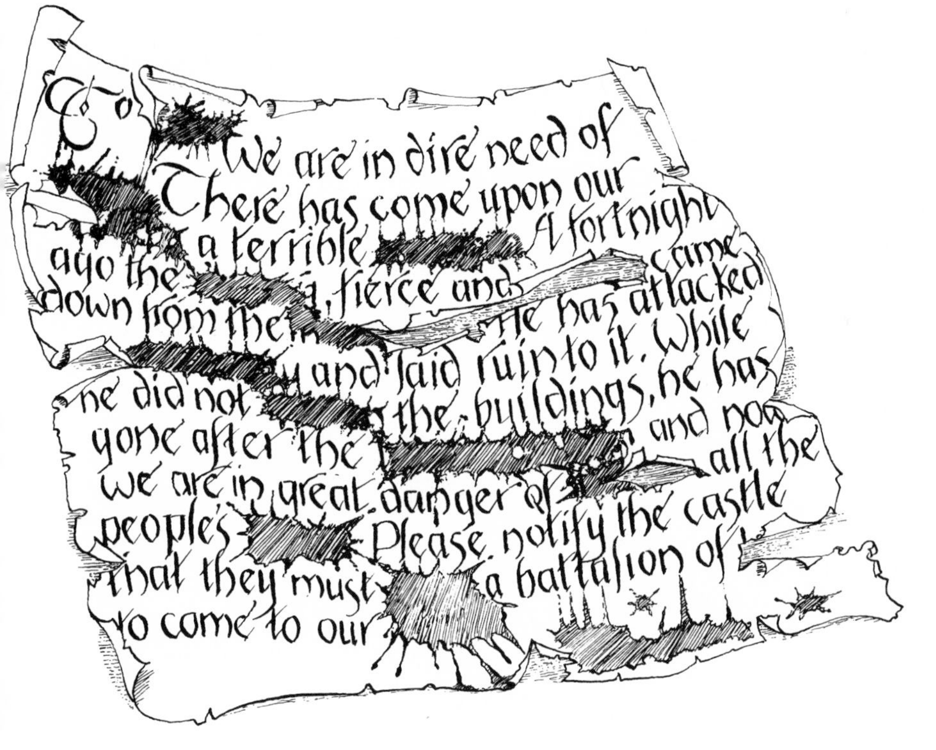

To
We are in dire need of
There has come upon our
a terrible A fortnight
ago the , fierce and came
down from the He has attacked
and laid ruin to it. While
he did not the buildings, he has
gone after the and now
we are in great danger of all the
people's Please notify the castle
that they must a battalion of
to come to our

The rain had played havoc with the message, wiping out so many words that it was quite impossible to decipher. Even the sender's name was gone.

"Sigfried? I hate to bother you," I said, "but I really do think you should look at this. The rain has smeared the ink and the message is so blurred you can't make out what it says."

Sigfried laid down his awl and looked at me. I could tell I'd aroused his curiosity. "After all," I went on, "you have had a lot of experience with blotches and such. Not that I'm being critical, of course, it's just that this may be a way to redeem yourself in the eyes of the armarius."

"There is, I suppose, some sort of . . . what's the word? . . . oh, logic in what you say," Sigfried agreed. "It cannot hurt to look at it, I suppose."

He picked up the parchment and began to read aloud: "'We are in dire need of something. There has come upon our something a terrible something. A fortnight ago the something, fierce and something came down from the something. He has attacked something something and laid ruin to it. While he did not something the buildings, he has gone after the something and now we are in great danger of something all the people's something. Please notify the castle that they must something a battalion of something to come to our something. Signed, Someone.'

"Well, *something* is certainly wrong with *someone,*" Sigfried said.

"Yes, but can you make out any of the blotched words?" I asked.

"No, we will have to guess at what they might be. Oh, my, what a daun . . . daun . . . well, difficult task. I am such a . . . a . . . whosits with words, you know."

"We can't just fill in *any* words," I said, somewhat shocked. "How would we know they were the right ones? You can't just plug a word in anywhere, just because you like the sound of it, or you haven't heard it lately. You couldn't, for instance, say 'We are in dire need of a rhinoceros,' just because it is your favorite word. What an absurd idea, Sigfried."

"Yes, it would be absurd to say . . . how-doyacallit . . . rhinoceros because the chances are they wouldn't write to the castle to get one," Sigfried said.

"But that's not the point," I said. I could not believe how dim-witted this human seemed about some things, particularly words. "There are over 350,000 words in my dictionary at home. We can't just keep plugging them in until we find one that we like."

"What is a dictionary?"

"Oh, never mind. In any case it's impossible."

"But it's not. I mean we should be able to narrow down the possi . . . possi . . . choices. After all, we know that *rhinoceros* is absurd. Now we must look at the whole message, what we have of it, that is, and see if we can figure out the meaning of the thing."

"This will never work," I told him, walking back up his sleeve and positioning myself in his hood. I had already read the thing twice and I could not make heads or tails of it. It was simply a jumble of words to me. But he insisted on going on with it, and I decided that my prodigious vocabulary might very well come in handy, so I went along.

CHAPTER 6

Of Sigfried's Extraordinary and Unaccountable Decision

"FIRST OF ALL," BEGAN SIGFRIED, POINTING TO the parchment, "we know they are in dire need of something. But I don't think we can figure out what that is until we determine what their . . . their . . . dinguswhatsis is."

"Their predicament you mean?" I asked.

"Yes, precisely. Now then, something has come upon their something. I would guess it is *village* or *hamlet* or *homes* or something to that effect. And whatever it is, it is not good."

Reading over Sigfried's shoulder, I filled in

the words. "*There has come upon our village a terrible*, not-so-good something."

"And whatever it is, it is fierce and lives in the mountains," Sigfried added. "Now it could be a wild animal of some sort, or an ogre maybe, or perhaps even a dragon, but it is so fierce and something that it has attacked them and laid ruin to something."

Taking Sigfried's guesses, I read on. "*A fortnight ago the* ogre, say, *fierce and* . . . what would an ogre be? Ugly maybe? OK, an ogre fierce and ugly came down from the mountains. *He has attacked* . . . what did we say before? Oh yes, village . . . *He has attacked our village and laid ruin to it.*"

"But he didn't hurt the buildings," Sigfried said, going on. "He's gone after something else, and now all the people are in danger of losing it. What on earth could it possibly be?"

I tried to figure it out before Sigfried. "Gold maybe?"

"Possibly," Sigfried said. "But people in a

village are not very likely to have a great deal of gold lying about."

"How about food?" I said. "If it is an ogre, wouldn't he be hungry? Maybe he's eaten everyone's food."

"Good guess," Sigfried said. "Let us continue. They want us to notify the castle to send a . . . a whowhatsis?"

"That's battalion," I said, reading over his shoulder.

"Oh yes. Well, it must be *knights,* for what else would make a battalion?"

And then I had it! "Of course," I said, "the first line. They need *help*. They need to be rescued. We must take this to the armarius as quickly as possible."

"But the castle will be of no help," Sigfried said. "All of the knights are away at a tournament. They will have no one to send."

"That's awful," I said. "But we must hurry! We'll take it to the armarius and he'll know what to do." I was practically shouting in Sigfried's ear.

"Let us not act too hastily," Sigfried said.

"Perhaps there is something we might be able to do. Perhaps this is the opportunity I have been waiting for all of my life. Perhaps I should go after this wild beast or ogre or dragon or whatever it is."

I could not believe what I was hearing. "Sigfried, that is absurd. You aren't a knight. You are a scribe. And not even a very good scribe. You can't just go gallivanting off after who knows what!"

"But it is what I have always wanted. I am not a good scribe because I don't want to be one. But if desire and willingness have anything to do with success, I know I could succeed as a knight."

"But Sigfried, you can't become a knight in a day," I said.

"That I know," Sigfried said. "But when I was a lad, I spent many hours listening to the local troubadour spin marvelous tales about the heroic deeds of knights. I feel as if I have been on many a quest myself, even if it was only through stories."

"Well, there is a big difference between

listening to stories or reading about something and actually doing it," I said, quite reasonably. Then I laughed. "But if that's true, what am I doing here?"

"You mean this is all part of a story?" Sigfried asked. "How interesting! You know, I have often had a feeling of . . . of . . . oh, blather . . . oh yes, of being carried away by a story. That is what has happened to you. So you are reading a story and I am in it. How interesting," he said again.

"Sigfried," I said, jarring him from his reverie, "let's get on with it."

"Oh yes, of course."

"Where are you going?" I asked as he got up and headed for the door.

"To the cellar, then on to glory!" he said.

"That wasn't the *it* I had in mind," I mumbled as I clung to the side of the hood, wondering what I was getting myself into.

Through the damp, dark corridors we went, and down and around circular stone staircases until I thought I would get quite dizzy. At last we reached the cold, dreary monastery cellar.

"You know," I said, "it is one thing to act on an impulse. But I think if you give it some thought you will see that this is a ridiculous idea. Let's go back, Sigfried. No one will ever be the wiser."

"You do not understand at all, do you, my small friend? There is an old English . . . uh . . . hootmalalie . . . you know, a proverb, that says 'A man of words and not of deeds is like a garden full of weeds.' Well, I have been overrun with words too long, and they always get the better of me."

I sighed. It was one thing for him to go chasing some foolhardy dream. But it didn't look as if I could stay behind if I kept reading. I had to try once more to change his mind and the direction in which the story seemed to be headed.

"Sigfried, you don't even know for sure what we are up against," I said. "Don't you think we should wait until we get more information?"

"By then, it may be too late."

We stopped before a heavy iron-barred door. "This must be it." Sigfried lifted the latch and pushed the door. The hinges creaked in protest as it slowly gave way. Sigfried took a torch from a bracket and we entered.

"What are we doing here?" I asked.

"Some of the monks were knights before they entered the monastery. Their old armor and weapons are stored down here someplace."

It must have been a long time since those knights had become monks. When Sigfried swung his torch over the width of the room, all I could see was a pile of broken and rusty armor, covered with dust and cobwebs.

I thought this would put a damper on Sigfried's enthusiasm, but he said, "Let us see if anything can be salv . . . salv . . . gotten from this."

What Sigfried was looking through was hardly what I might consider *armor*. When I saw that word, I envisioned a solid, impenetrable suit of metal. Sigfried found nothing but a helmet with a loose visor, a chain-mail shirt with a gaping hole through the front, a pair of gloves with two fingers missing, one full greave, and a bent, rusty shield.

Over in a corner he discovered a pair of moth-eaten trousers. "And this," Sigfried said, "will make me a shirt." He picked up a broken sword and hacked away at the bottom of his robe until it was short enough to tuck into the trousers. Then he tried on the various pieces, careful to leave his hood outside for me to ride in.

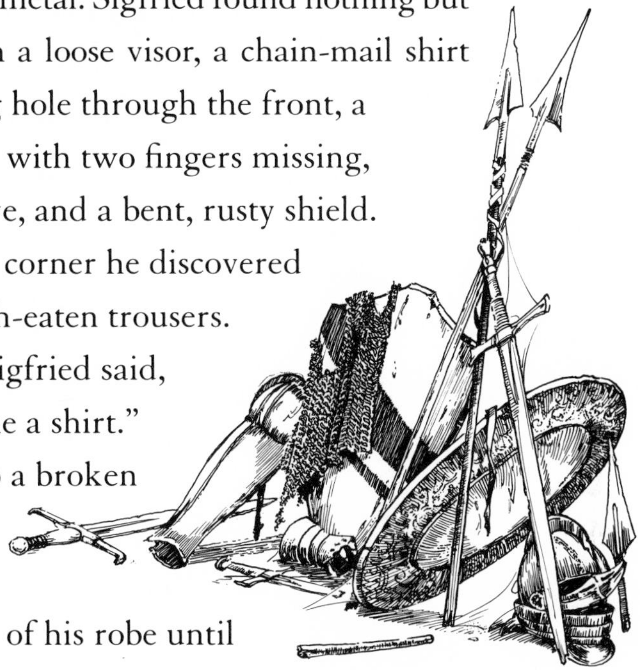

When I saw how ridiculous he looked, I thought it might be best to get out of this story immediately. I told Sigfried I was not going to go on.

"Oh, stay with me, my friend," he said. "How can you consider quitting just as our adventure gets started? And where would you go?"

That was something I hadn't thought about. If I quit reading I would wind up back in the bookstore, and I'd be right back in the thick of my own problems. And, while I wasn't sure I knew how Sigfried's story was going to turn out, I was curious to see if my guesses were correct.

"All right," I agreed reluctantly. "I will stay for a while, but do not expect me around for the bloody end."

Creaking and clanking with every step, we headed back upstairs.

"Now I must find a noble steed to carry me to victory," Sigfried said, opening another door. I was not prepared for the blast of bright light that poured through the opening.

CHAPTER 7

A Most Singular and Strange Adventure Befalls Sigfried

HAVING GROWN UP IN THE BOOKSTORE, THIS WAS my first experience with the outdoors, and I was having trouble making out what I was seeing. The sunlight was so bright . . . so much brighter than the fluorescent store lights, or the torches in the monastery. Or the word *sun* itself.

And the colors were all so vivid! Everything in the bookstore was muted and dusty, and the monastery had been mostly gray stone. But out here, the ground all around was brilliant green, and the sky the most beautiful blue. Huge, dark mounds rose up in the distance, and Sigfried told me those were mountains. They were quite impressive, until I remembered—that was where the ogre or dragon or whatever lived.

We made our way across a courtyard to another building, this one made of wood.

"There should be something here in the stables," Sigfried said. He pushed the door open, and before us was the biggest animal I'd ever seen. A hundred times bigger than the cat, it stood as tall as Sigfried himself. But for some strange reason, I wasn't the least bit frightened of it. There was something in the way it stood there, glancing at us out of half-closed eyes and then dropping its gray muzzle back into the box of grain, that made it very nonthreatening.

"Nothing here but this swaybacked old mule," Sigfried said. "He will have to do. I shall saddle him quickly and then we will be on our way." He tried to coax the reluctant mule from its supper, and only with a great struggle was he able to get the mule ready.

Mounting the mule was another battle. Sigfried tried to lift his leg to the stirrup, but the rusty armor would not bend enough. He went round to the other side of the mule and stepped up with his free leg. The weight of the armor threw him off balance, and we went crashing off the other side. Only by digging into the soft folds of Sigfried's hood with my nails did I escape being thrown to the ground.

At last, with the help of several crates, we were able to get into the saddle. Then we headed out of the main gate of the monastery, clanking with every step.

For a long time we plodded along through pages of empty country. I must admit I finally gave up trying to read and fell asleep. When I woke up I could see that we were approaching a small village. Could this be our destination?

I looked all around for signs of destruction and ruin, but could see nothing out of the ordinary.

"Sigfried, do you think this is it?" I asked.

"We will soon find out," Sigfried said. "Although everything appears to be quite normal."

The streets were full of bustling people, but as we passed by they stopped what they were doing and simply stared. Sigfried made quite a spectacle in his scrappy armor, riding an ancient mule. I was glad to be in his hood where no one could see me. And then it occurred to me that since no one could see me, they must think Sigfried was talking to himself.

"Perhaps I will not have to fight whatever it is after all," Sigfried said. "Perhaps it will take one look at me and laugh itself to death."

I did not find anything funny in his remark, but I said nothing for fear our conversation was making Sigfried appear even more ridiculous.

"Cervantes? . . . Cervantes?"

But as I refused to answer, he at last gave up on me.

When we got to the town square, a group of burly men approached us, and I pulled myself deeper into the folds of the hood. *This is it,* I thought. *They will run us out of town.*

They stood blocking our way, and the largest and meanest-looking one began to speak.

Don't be too harsh on my poor, foolish friend, I wanted to tell him.

But when he spoke, I was caught off guard.

"You have come," he said. "Just in the nick of impatience. At present there are such goings on that everything is at a standstill."

I could not have read that right. "What did he say?" I whispered to Sigfried.

"I do not have a clue," Sigfried whispered back. "It seems this helmet has affected my hearing." He leaned over toward the man and said, "How may I be of ser . . . ser . . . oh, what can I do for you?"

"You cannot," the man said. "If you do not save us we shall surely survive."

"He's not making any sense," I said. "And words are supposed to make sense. Sigfried, we must get away from here." But the man had a hold of the mule's reins. I could see we weren't going anywhere.

Just then, another man spoke. "We sent to the king for a knight and he doesn't give us the time of day. This is magnificent; all is lost."

"Perhaps we would get on better," Sigfried said, "if you would just start at the beginning."

"This is the lad to tell it," another man said, pushing a boy toward Sigfried. "He has no idea where to begin."

The boy stepped up beside us. He was dressed, not like the others in working clothes, but in a pale gray tunic. Around his waist was wrapped a bright purple sash with long fringe.

"He is a troubadour's apprentice," Sigfried whispered. "The more stories they know, the more colored stripes on their sash. He must be very new."

As he began to talk, the boy's hands flew around as if he were groping for the right words.

"Now, there is nothing to tell, and it is a long tale," the boy said. "Listen well, for I am going to tell you something I know nothing about. It all happened a long time ago, no later than yesterday." Though he was a boy he spoke with great authority.

"We were on our way here, to Newcastle,

having arrived the day before. These people had asked the troubadours to tell their stories at a festival, after it was over. You see, it is traditional for them to set aside a week in June for their winter carnival, though this is the first time they have ever done it."

"Go on, go on," the men shouted. "Say no more."

"As we were about to begin our performance it began to pour. The sun shone brightly on the rain, and everyone was forced to seek shelter in an open field. As we stood, sitting on the grass, there suddenly appeared before us a colossal dragon, right behind us."

"Why, if St. George were alive, he would have turned over in his grave," a man shouted.

The boy nodded and continued. "I was frightened to life and I concluded in the beginning that this would be the end of it, and I see I was right, for it is not half over yet.

"Upon seeing us," he went on, "the dragon let out such a mighty roar that the silence echoed all around. I was, to put it in two words, horrified! The dragon told us he was Censor, the meanest in the land, and then I heard him say, though I did not hear a word of it, that we must forfeit our gold or our lives. The troubadours had to be honest, so they lied through their teeth and told him we had nothing to give. They explained that they were complete nobodies, only the finest storytellers in all the land.

"Well, the dragon took their meaning all wrong and figured out what they were saying. 'So, it is your stories that make you all so worthless?' and the troubadours had to agree, though they knew he was mistaken."

I was so baffled by now, I sighed loudly.

Apparently the boy did not hear me, but continued his strange story. "'Then that is what I will take from you,' the dragon concluded, not being finished with us yet. Kneeling, the troubadours begged him on straightened knee not to take their stories, and the dragon gave his word, then took all the words right out of their mouths. But the stories were strong. The dragon left us here and flew to the Moralise Mountains with all of the troubadours but me." The boy hung his head sadly.

"As you can see quite darkly, we are all in total confusion," said one of the men. "Every one of us was left speaking nothing but tangle-talk. All the stories of the people, the folktales, fairy tales, myths, and legends are safe with the troubadours, as they may lose them all to the dragon. This is such a wonderful mess we have just gotten out of!"

CHAPTER 8

That Gives an Account of Things That You'll Know When You Read It

"This is as bad as the note with the missing words," I whispered to Sigfried.

"Yes, but I think if we take what we know from the note, and add whatever we can from this 'tangle-talk,' we may end up with some answers," Sigfried said, looking at the men. They stared back at him.

"Oh, this is just the beginning," cried one of them. "It is all over. This so-called knight includes us out when he speaks. The dragon has turned his mind to clarity."

"They think you are as mixed-up as they are," I whispered to Sigfried.

"At the moment, I am," he said.

"Come, fellows," the man said, letting go of the reins and backing away. "Don't pay any attention to this man, don't even ignore him." They walked away, arguing amongst themselves.

Soon we were alone in the street. "There is proof of your folly," I told Sigfried. "Even those mumjummers have no faith in you."

"Cervantes, you are becoming a real dry-asdust. This is the eleventeenth time you have wanted to quit," Sigfried said. "Have you no sense of adventure, no imagination? There is much work to be done. Either you are in or you are out. But you must make the decision now whether the story stops here or goes on."

If I stopped, this story could not go on without me. I could see how much this whole knighthood thing meant to Sigfried. Maybe some of his foolishness was wearing off on me, I don't know. But for some reason I was feeling more intrigued than frightened, and so I said, "Let the story continue," and kept on reading.

"The first order of business then," Sigfried responded, "is to take a look at the note and see if we can fill in any of the missing . . . missing . . . dodibbles."

"Words, you mean."

"Oh yes, words." Sigfried reached into the pocket of the pant leg without armor and pulled out the note. He struggled to see through the visor.

"It is no use, I cannot see through this . . . thingaswhatsis . . . this contraption," he said. He raised it up, but it clanked down again over his face.

"Riggafrutch!" he exclaimed, raising it up and holding it there.

I quickly crawled up on the helmet and braced myself against the plume holder on top, grasping the visor with my tail.

"There, now I can manage. *We are in dire need of* something," Sigfried read. "Well, we decided before that was help. *We are in dire need of help. There has come upon our* village, obviously, *a terrible* . . . what?"

"Disaster," I said. "It is clear from what they told us that it is a *disaster* or a *calamity* or some such word."

"Yes. *There has come upon our village a*

terrible disaster. A fortnight ago the—and now we know for certain what it was. It was not an ogre or a wild animal, but a dragon—*dragon, fierce and ferocious, came down from the mountains. He has attacked our community and laid ruin to it. While he did not* . . . what to the buildings?"

I looked around at the village, but I couldn't see anything that had been harmed. "It must be *harm,*" I said, filling it in. "*While he did not harm the buildings, he has gone after* . . . oh, what did that boy call them . . . the ones who tell tales?"

"The troubadours," Sigfried said. *"He has gone after the troubadours and now we are in great danger of losing all the people's . . . stories."*

"There, now we have the facts. But surely you must realize that you cannot go after a dragon by yourself. We need help."

"St. George did not need help and neither do I. Besides, I have you to constantly remind me of the . . . thingamawhatsises . . . the dangers," Sigfried said, spurring on his mule, who merely turned around and nipped him on his unarmored leg.

"Onward to the Moralise Mountains," Sigfried cried, but the mule stood stock-still. "Come on, you ragabash old mule. You must hurry."

The mule did not budge.

"Apparently it is not moved by the urgency," Sigfried said, as he rattled his armor and jounced up and down on the mule's back. But it stood rooted to the ground.

"You uzzihamper, you twittlewattle, you . . . oh, what am I going to do?"

"Perhaps it's waiting for the magic word?" I suggested. After all, the mule was just an animal, like me or the cat, only bigger. And I knew what motivated the cat and me.

"Magic word? Yes, perhaps that would work. Now let me think, magic words . . . all right. *Abracadabra.*"

But the mule did not move. I wanted to make a suggestion, but I could not get a word in edgewise as Sigfried rambled on.

"How about *ofano, oblamo, ospergo?* No? Well then, *pax, sax, sarax! Afa, afca, nostra?* How about *hocus pocus?*"

Nothing seemed to have any effect on the mule. "How about—" I began, but Sigfried cut me short.

"Oh, I know a good one," Sigfried said. "It is supposed to be the spell that witches use when they mount their broomsticks:

Horse and hattock,
Horse and go,
Horse and pelatis,
Ho, ho!

He yelled, but the mule stood fast.

I couldn't take it any longer, and I just skipped down the page to where Sigfried finally gave up.

"Oh, this is hopeless," he cried. "This old whatchamacallit is never going to move"

"How about *food,*" I finally managed to blurt out.

"That is silly. *Food?*" And as Sigfried said the word, the mule pricked up its ears and started plodding slowly up the street.

"Well, I never! Who would have thought such a common word could work magic?"

CHAPTER 9

Of the Ominous Accidents That Crossed Sigfried as He Entered the Forest

As we rode out of the village square, Sigfried looked about for someone to give him directions. But there was not another soul in sight.

"This is quite odd," Sigfried said. "There were so many people out and about when we rode into town. Where could they all have gone? The dragon must have these poor folks deathly afraid."

I did not want to say anything, but I wondered if it was the dragon who frightened them, or Sigfried in his ridiculous getup, talking to himself.

Luckily for us, there was a signpost at the edge of town, and one of the signs said *Moralise Mountains* and was pointing in the direction of a dense thicket of trees. I figured that this must be a *forest*.

The closer we got to the forest, the more foreboding it appeared. The tangle of branches shut out the sun, so everything was dark and shadowy, reminding me of the cold stone passages of the monastery.

The moment we entered the forest, it felt cold and damp and there was a funny smell in the air, quite different from the dry, dusty smell of old books. This was a rich, decaying scent that made my whiskers twitch.

"Are you certain we have to go through this forest?" I asked.

"You saw the signpost in town. This most definitely is the . . . the . . . dingus whatsis that goes to the Moralise Mountains."

"But it is so—" Just then a great dark bird swooped down on us from the trees, squawking. The mule flinched then bolted straight into the woods. It went at top speed through the tangled trees, Sigfried clinging to its back and me clinging to Sigfried's hood, until a low-hanging branch swept us both from the saddle like a blow from a lance.

When we landed, I quickly crawled out of the hood. Sigfried got up and started stumbling around blindly, shouting, "Everything's gone black!"

And there above me was the visor of Sigfried's helmet.

"Oh no, Sigfried. Your head is on backward!" I cried.

"It is? Oh, this is . . . this is . . . well, whatever it is, it is dreadful. Yes, that is it, dreadful," he said. "What am I going to do? Hindsight is not very useful if you are trying to move ahead."

Feeling the helmet with his hands Sigfried said, "No, wait! It is not my head that is screwed on wrong after all. It is the helmet." He tried to turn it around, but it wouldn't budge. "Oh, dear, what an awful doojigger I have gotten myself into now!"

Suddenly a shadow fell across us and a booming voice echoed from above. "Your precipitant actions may hasten your untimely demise!"

The voice was human, but it seemed to be coming from the treetops. Then the earth started to shake as whatever it was came closer.

I was absolutely terrified. I dove into the dark folds of Sigfried's hood. I didn't want to read on, but I could hardly leave my friend here in this wilderness with his helmet screwed on backward and who knows what kind of monster coming for us. So at first, whenever that awful voice boomed out, I just read through the line as quick as I could, hardly noticing the words at all.

Sigfried, however, didn't seem the least bit frightened by the voice because he called out,

"Oh, wonderful, there is someone out there. Hello?"

"It appears that you have entangled yourself in quite a predicament. Would my assistance facilitate your removal from this unpropitious situation?" asked the boomer.

"I am not sure who you are or what you are talking about, but if you could just help me get this infandous helmet off my head, I would be most grateful," Sigfried said.

"Elementary," roared the voice, and as it spoke something came crashing down on Sigfried's head and the helmet split in two and fell to the ground. I crawled up just far enough to see if Sigfried's head had also split open and found myself looking at a wide expanse of coarse blue material. Glancing down I saw a humongous boot, the top of which came up to Sigfried's head. Then I looked up, and up, and up. . . .

"A giant!" Sigfried cried, without hesitation.

"Jargon the Giant, you nigmenog. You certainly are given to perspicuous deductions."

I stopped reading. Even a master of the dictionary like me can find some words just too dense to get past. I was hopelessly bogged down in *perspicuous deductions*. I could feel myself slipping out of the story; I couldn't see giant or forest or even Sigfried, just those two big words.

And then, there I was, back in the bookstore, on the pages of Sigfried's tale. I didn't really want to leave him, but I was exhausted from trying to wade through the giant's talk. So I sat there, trying to find a way back in, but I kept reading the same paragraph over and over again. Looking farther down the page, I saw that there were more big words, so I gave up.

I settled right down in the crease of the book and let my heavy eyelids fall shut. But even sleep could not get Sigfried's story out of my head.

I dreamed that Sigfried was in another forest, only this time the trees were actually words and every way he turned they blocked his path. He whirled round and round, trying to see a way through the thick verbiage, but there was no way out. He was calling to me, but he couldn't hear my answer. I slept on and on.

CHAPTER 10

The Never-to-Be-Imagined Combat Between Jargon and the Valorous Sigfried

WHEN I FINALLY WOKE UP I WAS SWEATING AND shaking all over. I rushed back to the page where I had left off and tried to find my place. I could not stand the suspense. And then I saw them, the two big words that had forced me out of the story before—*perspicuous deductions*.

They seemed just as impenetrable. But then I remembered my experience in the passage of the monastery when I'd first started this book. I'd come up against that other word I didn't know—*scriptorium*. And I had finally gotten past it by just slipping through it. However, these words seemed different. What if the giant were saying something really important—something we needed to understand in order not to be killed?

The only way to find out was to go on with the story and see what happened. I could skim over the giant's words and see if I could get anything from them. If I really needed to understand what he was saying, I could go back later and try to puzzle it out.

I found the sentence with *perspicuous deductions* and skipped over it, getting back into the story just in time to hear Sigfried ask, "What is it that you want from me?"

The giant's voice bellowed. "I was hoping for a stimulating verbal exchange, but it is apparent that you are too much of a puzzlepate for that. Perhaps you would serve as good bellytimber."

"Do you mean to eat me?" Sigfried asked, jumping back.

"I would if my appetite were more voracious. But I am no gundygut. My gastronomical satiety has arrived at a state of surfeit, and you would be nothing more than lubberwort anyway."

"Oh, good, I am glad," Sigfried said. He had no more idea of what lubberwort was than I did, but we were both glad he was one.

"Since you do not wish to eat me, may I pass and get on with my . . . my thingamajig?" Sigfried asked.

"Your vocabulary seems sadly deficient. Get on with your what?"

"My . . . my . . . oh yes, my quest." Sigfried said.

"Quest, is it? So that is your motive for gongoozeling around my forested habitat."

"Yes, I am on my way to the Moralise Mountains. I must find Censor the dragon and save the troubadours."

"Dragon slaying, is it?" Jargon roared with

laughter, and the trees all around shook as if there were a fierce storm. "You dunderwhelp! Your preparation for the encounter is pretty paltry. Is that dishabille of metallic apparel supposed to protect you?"

Sigfried looked down at his sorry suit of armor, the word "metallic" having been a sort of clue. "I plan to use my wits against him," he said.

"You are nothing but a blatherskite. The dragon will frighten the wits right out of you, then annihilate you."

"I do not scare so easily," Sigfried said.

I had to admit his B★R★A★V★E W★O★R★D★S seemed to have some merit. Jargon's big vocabulary was still a bit intimidating to me, even though I was just skimming. But Sigfried didn't seem the least bit frightened and I began to have new respect for him.

The giant was not impressed. "Courageous talk for such a clumperton. But, I shall examine your wits and logodaedaly with an ambage, and we will discover if you possess the facetiae necessary to vanquish the dragon. If you wish to continue through my weald, you must first unravel this riddle. What is the longest word in the English language?"

A riddle. And about words. If Sigfried had to answer it alone, we were doomed. His only hope was me. I thought back to my wall and the two words that were its foundation. "Try *antidisestablishmentarianism,*" I said.

But the giant just scoffed at Sigfried's attempt. His snorting laugh let loose a great blast of putrid air.

What horrible bad breath, I thought, burying my nose in the folds of the hood.

"Now try *floccinaucinihilipilification,*" I told Sigfried, quickly covering my nose again.

Once again, the giant only laughed.

"But it has to be one of them," I told Sigfried. "He is trying to trick us."

"You would not be cheating, would you?" asked Sigfried.

"Have you the audacity to doubt my veracity and insinuate that I prevaricate, you whiffet?" roared Jargon, leering at us.

"Sigfried, what is he talking about?" I asked.

"I do not have a clue. Up until now I have got the gist of what he was saying, but that last one has left me completely bam . . . bam . . . bamboozled."

"Well, *do* something," I yelled fiercely in his ear. "He is going to completely overwhelm us with his big words."

"Nonsense," Sigfried said. "It is his failure, not ours." Sigfried shouted up to the giant. "You cannot impress me with your . . . your bafflegab. You could say twice as much in half the time if you used smaller words, and you would make a lot more sense."

"But it is a man's manner of speech that defines him," the giant bellowed.

"Not so," Sigfried said. "It is his ability to be understood that makes the difference. I know of scribes at the scriptorium who make their letters so fancy, with so many extra flourishes and curlicues that, while they are very pretty to look at, they are impossible to read. So they have defeated their whole purpose in writing. You are doing the same in your speech."

"Yes, but if you have difficulty deciphering my sesquipedalian language, then you must be even more intimidated by my magnitudinous appearance."

I had been thinking about what Sigfried had said and could see now what he meant when he said it was the giant's failure and not ours. What was the point of talking if you were doing nothing more than trying to confuse someone? In spite of the way Sigfried stumbled over his words, I could see he had good, upstanding ideas.

Sigfried pulled the broken sword from his belt. "It is time to cut through all your nonsense. You are nothing but a lot of hot air. And the answer to your riddle is *smiles* because there is a mile between the two *s*'s."

He thrust the sword into the giant's leg,

and his SHORT, PRECISE WORDS made the point even sharper. When the blade pierced the giant's skin, a great gust of air blew out of the hole, knocking us to the ground and toppling trees all around us.

When the wind stopped, Sigfried picked me up off the ground and replaced me in his hood. We looked all around for the giant, but he was gone, and in his place stood a small troll, who was snuffling and rubbing his eyes with his fists.

"You are so mean," he cried. "You have poked holes in my argument and now look at me!" And he went sniveling away into the forest.

As I watched him go, I felt foolish for having been so frightened of him. I could see now how empty his big words had been.

But instead of being relieved, I had a kind of queasy feeling in my stomach. First of all, my big vocabulary had not helped one bit. Sigfried had defeated the giant on his own. And what's more, hadn't I relied on big words to build my wall back in the bookstore? If they really didn't mean much. . . . I couldn't bear to think about it. Besides, Sigfried had found his mule and mounted. For the first time, we saw a clear path leading out of the tangled woods.

CHAPTER II

What Befell the Renowned Adventurers in the Fearful Moralise Mountains

WE RODE ON THROUGH THE AFTERNOON. FOR A while I didn't pay much attention to where we were. I kept thinking about our encounter with the giant and what it all meant. It seemed now that all the big words I had used as a defense against the cat were really quite senseless. But I didn't have a clue what I could protect myself with instead. I had been pondering the problem for a long time before I noticed we had stopped moving.

"This is no time to quit reading," Sigfried said. "We are almost to our destination."

I went back and read the last paragraph to get my bearings. We were on the crest of a hill, and rising before us was a very strange mountain.

I was quite used to mountains by now and knew them to be large and jagged and very green. But this one was charcoal black and the top was surrounded by clouds, and not the kind of fluffy white clouds I had become accustomed to, either. They were a sinister, grayish brown, rising up from the slopes of the smoldering peak.

"I believe we have found Censor's home," Sigfried said, pointing to the smoke clouds. I felt a shiver run up his spine. "It is more horrible than I had imagined."

"Have you got a plan?" I asked.

"No, I want to get a closer look. You are not thinking of abandoning me now, are you?"

Actually, I *had* thought about it. But when I tried to tear my eyes from the page I found I couldn't. I was much too involved in the story to stop reading.

"No, I am with you all the way," I replied.

"Excellent," Sigfried said.

I noticed that Sigfried was not tripping over words as much. First *destination,* then *horrible, imagined, abandoning,* and now *excellent.* I was about to remark on it when I noticed an awful smell. It reminded me of a hunk of rotten egg-salad sandwich that one of the bookstore customers had dropped by the reference section once. By now, the black soot had started clinging to Sigfried's armor, turning him a dusty gray.

When we reached the base of the peak, the mule once again stopped. "Come on, you old jabbernowl! Food! We will find you some food!" But this time the mule was not moved at all by Sigfried's plea.

"I guess we might as well leave the mule here. The mountain looks pretty steep and rocky."

We dismounted and Sigfried began the arduous climb. The higher we went, the stinkier it got. We began to hear a low rumbling noise that seemed to come from the heart of the mountain itself.

"What is that?" I asked.

Sigfried looked up and searched the mountainside. "There," he said, pointing directly above us. "That hole with the smoke coming from it. That must be the dragon's lair. And that sounds like snoring."

"Why would a dragon be asleep during the day?" I asked.

"So he can fight knights, I suppose," Sigfried answered. "Maybe we can sneak up on him before he awakens."

"Well, we'll never be able to sneak up with all your clanging and clattering."

Sigfried stopped and, with a loud clunk, sat down on a rock. "You are right. Anyway, it is so hot inside this armor that I will melt before we get there. It must come off."

"But won't you need it when you meet the dragon?"

"I doubt if it's going to provide much protection from Censor's flames. I would just cook like a roast in an oven."

"Well, *hurry,* before he wakes up."

Sigfried lifted me from his hood and set me on a rock. I read fitfully as he seemed to take forever to get out of the armor. Finally, after much clattering, bumping, and thumping, the armor lay in a pile on the ground. I crawled up Sigfried's trouser leg and back into the hood.

As we climbed, the heat and the smell got worse. I had to keep flicking the sweat from my brow with my tail and pinching my nose shut with my paws. At last we reached the top of a large outcropping and together we peered over the other side, into the mouth of a large cave.

"I fear I cannot look closer," Sigfried said. "You go up yourself."

"Alone?" I cried. I had no intention of leaving the safety of Sigfried's hood, however tenuous that safety was.

"Read ahead then. Skip to the part where

the dragon is described and then come back and tell me what it says."

"I would have to leave you here alone," I reminded him.

"I will be fine, as long as the dragon stays sleeping. Hurry now."

So I left Sigfried crouching beneath the entrance to the cave and jumped ahead in the story, trying to find the description of the dragon.

I had no sooner found it than I came up against a fearsome-looking word. "The dragon, slimy and *squamous*." I had no idea what *squamous* meant, but the very word made my whiskers tremble in fear. I paused, then thought of Sigfried all alone a couple of pages back and knew that the dragon could awake at any moment. So I forced myself to read on. The picture that the words created was the most terrifying thing I had ever seen.

I don't know what I expected, but when we had first set out on this adventure I pictured a *dragon* as a sort of large, green cat. But now I realized that I could never have imagined anything as horrifying as the real thing.

He was big . . . much bigger than I'd thought possible. In fact, he was bigger than the giant. I could not even see the end of his tail, which was coiled into the murky depths of the cave. His nostrils were like two bright craters of molten lava. Their glow illuminated his grotesque head. The slimy scales that covered his body glistened like stagnant water. And his snores . . . his snores thundered in my ears. But worst of all were the waves of stench that rose from his body.

I quickly lifted my eyes from the page and away from that terrifying spectacle. Then I scurried back to the spot where I had left Sigfried waiting. I told him everything I'd seen—even the part about the dragon being squamous. When I'd finished Sigfried had gone all white, and with the soot on his face he looked very ghostly.

"Oh, dear," he said. "I had no idea. This was a very foolish scheme indeed. How are we

ever going to defeat a . . . a . . . so-and-so like that?"

"We?" I said. "I am just going along for the ride. I have no intention of fighting any dragon. I'm just the reader."

"But someone must save the troubadours or there will be no more stories. We have to think of something."

"How about going back and finding some *real* help?" I suggested.

"And where do you propose we find anyone? The knights will not be back for a fortnight, and those people in the village cannot even put two words together correctly. It is up to us."

"Us?" I squeaked.

Sigfried ignored me. "The first thing we must do is think about what we know of dragons. Over the years at the monastery I have heard a good many tales of dragon slay-

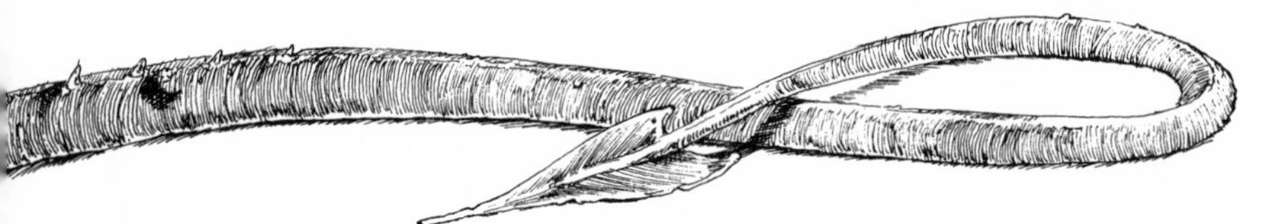

ing from the knights who brought us dragon's blood."

"Dragon's blood?" I cried. The very idea was ghoulish. "Why in the world would they bring you dragon's blood?"

"We use it to dissolve the gold paint for the illuminated manuscripts."

I thought back to those marvelous shining pictures and wondered how something so beautiful could have anything to do with something as disgusting as dragon's blood.

"I have learned from those stories that the breath of a dragon can be quite pois . . . pois . . . bad for you. But even more important, their burning gaze is certain death if you should look into their eyes."

"Well, since I have no intention of coming out of your hood, that won't be a problem for me," I said.

"But it will be for me . . . unless we can sneak past him while he is still asleep." Sigfried sighed.

"I'm for any plan that doesn't involve a lot

of violence and bloodshed." In spite of my misgivings, I was totally caught up in the story. "I'm willing to at least give it a try."

"We will have to enter the cave without any light. But once we get past him we will need torches to find the troubadours."

"Where will we get the torches?" I asked.

"Torches are made from wood and pitch."

I looked around at the charred and smoldering mountainside. "Where will we get that?"

"I guess we can return to the forest, make our torches, and then come back when we can once again hear the dragon's snores."

My heart sank. That seemed like a long, drawn-out process, and right when we had reached the climax of the story. Part of me wanted just to get on with it, to go into the cave and face the dragon head on. But if what Sigfried had said about dragons was true, the ending could be awfully quick. Another part of me wanted the story to go on forever. So at last I agreed, and we went back down the mountain to the mule, who seemed rather surprised to see us again.

Our torch making didn't take long and the entire procedure was uneventful. We waited until we heard the low rumblings of the dragon's snores again, and then we returned to the cave, armed only with two big pitch torches and our faltering courage.

Sigfried began to inch forward. His knees were shaking so badly that he wobbled dangerously on the loose rocks. I had to dig my nails into his hood with all my might to keep from being jiggled out.

Just as we got over the edge of the outcrop, Sigfried's legs gave way and, to our horror, we tumbled in a heap right under the dragon's nose.

The dragon stopped snoring, and slowly—very slowly—raised his head.

CHAPTER 12

Being an Account of Our Descent to the Darkest Depths

We dared not open our eyes for fear we might meet the deadly dragon gaze. But the dragon was only shifting positions in his sleep, because his head came back down, barely missing us. His snores once again shook the ground.

Neither one of us could breathe very well, and heat and fear were making us dizzy, but we waited a moment to make sure it was safe. Standing by the dragon's flaming nostrils, Sigfried reached out ever so carefully with one of the torches and lit the end of it. He nearly dropped the torch on the dragon's nose, his hand was shaking so. Holding the torch aloft, we crawled past the sleeping Censor.

Sigfried held a rag over his nose to lessen the terrible stench, and I burrowed deeper into the folds of his hood. Even so, the poisonous vapor stung our eyes.

Farther and farther into the cave we crept until even the sickly glow from the dragon's nostrils had long ago disappeared. Finally we saw the vague shapes of people slumped against the wall.

As we hurried over, I saw there were four of them: three men and a woman. Heavy, metal chains were wrapped around their feet like hobbles. They were dressed like the boy in town, in pale gray tunics. But the sashes around their waists were brightly colored with many stripes.

Sigfried approached the closest one, a portly man with flowing white hair and a beard, and tapped him gently on the shoulder. Startled, the man blinked a few times and then seemed to notice us.

"Who are you, young man? Another troubadour captured to share our fate?" he asked. At the sound of his voice, the others seemed to rise up out of their stupor.

"Oh, no. I am no troubadour. I am the knight who has come to rescue you. Well, no, that is not exactly true," Sigfried said, knowing that no one could see through a story faster than a storyteller. "I am merely a scribe at a monastery. But, you see, I happened to meet one of your apprentices, and he was searching for a knight to rescue you."

Another of the troubadours leaned forward. Her sash was a brilliant rainbow of colors and even the dull torchlight could not diminish its glow. "I am Barda," she said. "The lad was my apprentice. I saw that he had escaped Censor's notice. He must not have known enough stories yet for Censor to bother with him. He will not be able to save our tales."

"But did you hear that, Columba?" asked the youngest troubadour, turning to the white-haired troubadour.

"Hear what, Goliard?"

"There are knights coming to our rescue!"

"No, not exactly knights," Sigfried said. "You see, the castle knights were away at a tournament, so I have come in their stead."

Columba smiled sadly. "That was very brave of you, young scribe. But as you can see, even knights would face an impossible task here. These chains make it impossible to get past Censor. We are doomed." He slumped back against the wall.

"But there must be a way to release you."

"Not from *these* chains. Censor has taken our own words, cast them in iron, and twisted them all around until they bind us fast. He is determined to keep us here in the dark until we have forgotten our stories."

"But I do not understand why the dragon wants your stories in the first place," Sigfried said.

"Tell him, Chaucer," Barda said, turning to the thin, gaunt man next to her.

"He fears them greatly," Chaucer said. "He knows how powerful stories can be, and he does not want the people's minds 'fouled,' as he says, by tales of dragon slaying. He believes that if the people never hear of a dragon's defeat, they will think dragons are all-powerful."

"But why does he keep you trapped in his cave?" Sigfried asked. "Why does he not just reduce you to tangle-talk like he has the townsfolk?"

Chaucer looked up fiercely. "Because our stories are too strong. It will take a long time to make us forget them completely, even with the strength of Censor's poisonous breath. When we have forgotten the last fragments of the old stories he plans to fill our minds with his own tales of the invincibility of dragons."

"Then we must think of a way to free you before it is too late," Sigfried said.

"It is doubtless too late already," Columba said. "None of us can remember more than bits and pieces even now."

"But surely there is something . . ."

"No," Goliard said. "Give up, lad. You would be best advised to sneak out of here before the dragon wakes up. There is no reason for you to perish in Censor's flames as well."

Sigfried slumped to the floor before the troubadours. "Oh, how I have failed," he said. "Imagine me, a simple scribe thinking I had what it takes to be a knight. You must all think I am a fool."

At this point in the story I was tempted to reach up and whisper in Sigfried's ear, "I told you so." But I had become impressed over the pages with Sigfried's ability. "Be strong," I whispered into his ear.

"I am not strong, nor brave, nor gallant, and I never was," Sigfried said. "There was a point when I thought I might be strong and brave and gallant, or at least strong and brave, or brave and gallant, or gallant and strong, or if not brave and strong, or gallant and brave, or strong and gallant, at least strong, or brave, or gallant, without knowing it."

"It seems Censor's poisonous breath is having an effect on you already," Goliard said.

"Oh, no, I talk this way all the time. I have always had trouble with words. They slip through my mind too easily."

Suddenly, from far up in the cavern above us came a horrendous crackling sound. It echoed around the rock walls and seemed to go right through us. And just as suddenly, all was still. After some time, Barda spoke.

"That was only Censor yawning," she said, reaching out to Sigfried. "You are lucky this time, young scribe. But since you can do no good here, it is best that you get out while you can."

I could see that by now Sigfried had lost all his courage and confidence. "If you give up now," I whispered in his ear, "then this will end up being the story of your defeat by the invincible dragon. And if it turns out that way, then Censor will have won in more ways than one. We cannot let that happen."

"Do you have any brilliant ideas?" Sigfried asked. "I'm all out."

CHAPTER 13

Wheerein Sigfried Saves the Stories—Almost

I SCUTTLED FROM SIGFRIED'S SHOULDER BACK into his hood. I felt so let down that I couldn't think of anything more to say. To come all this way, to go through all the trials and tribulations we had, just to have the end be such a disappointment.

But Sigfried wasn't getting up to leave. In fact, he was saying something more to the bards and troubadours. I crawled back up to his shoulder to listen.

". . . and you said you still remember bits and pieces of the stories. Since there is no way I can get any of you out of here, I must try to get the stories out. I myself am a real dunderhead when it comes to storytelling. Most of the time I cannot remember the words I am going to say, much less a whole story, but I could write the stories down and sneak them out that way."

"That is a truly stupendous idea!" Chaucer said.

"And you thought you were out of them," I whispered.

"But wait," Barda said, her face falling. "What will you use? We have no parchment, no ink."

Sigfried was stunned. Obviously he hadn't thought of that.

But just then, one of my favorite words came to me. Before, I had just liked the way it sounded, but now its meaning excited me. "Improvise," I whispered in Sigfried's ear.

"Improvise?" he said aloud.

"Yes, of course," said Columba. "We could use the cloth from our over-tunics for parchment. It is too warm in this cave anyway."

"Wonderful idea!" said Chaucer. "I am willing to give the shirt off my back to save our stories. And the pitch from your torches melted down would make a fine, if somewhat sticky ink."

"Yes," Sigfried agreed, "and I could make a point out of one of those to use for a stylus," he said, pointing to the bones scattered on the cave floor. Quickly he began to make the necessary preparations.

Soon he had all the troubadours' tunics laid out on the floor of the cave. The pitch bubbled over a small fire made from the torch handles. My job was to gnaw the end of a bone to sharpen it.

"Have you got the point, Cervantes?" Sigfried asked.

"Yes," I said. "I think I am finally getting the point."

Sigfried tried writing a few letters with the

pitch. He got stuck on some when he went too slow and the pitch cooled, but all in all it seemed to work.

"Now," he said to the troubadours, "tell me what you remember."

". . . the knight's shield held a sharply spiked umbo, through the center of the escutcheon which . . ."

". . . and the wormstench overpowered him."

"Gonfalon flying, the army set off for . . ."

"The dragon, a robustious fellow, reared out of the bog. . . ."

"Stop! Stop!" Sigfried yelled.

"What is wrong, dear scribe? Are we talking too quickly? Why are you being such a laggard?"

Sigfried had not written a single word. He threw down his stylus. "Everything you are saying is twaddle and blather, fiddlefaddle and diddledaddle. What knight? What dragon? What army?" he cried in frustration.

The troubadours looked crestfallen. "It is

no use," Chaucer said sadly. "That is all we can remember, just fragments."

"Well, it is nothing but gibberish," Sigfried said. "My plan was a foolish one. Unless . . ." He paused and turned to me. "Cervantes, would you be willing to go back and forth through the pages, putting all the scraps into their proper order so you could dictate them to me?"

"And how will I know what order they go in?" I asked.

"You are nearly through with *this* story so you must have some idea of how a story should go," he said. "There is a beginning, usually, 'Once upon a time' or something like that. And then there is the middle where the hero must overcome certain obstacles in his path like the giant in this story. And then there is the big climax where he fights the dragon. And then the victorious end."

I had my doubts, but I knew I had to try. If we could not salvage the stories, Censor would win and even Sigfried's tale would have a disastrous finish. So I began my tedious work.

The troubadours spoke the pieces of their stories. I returned to the bookstore and flipped ahead in the book. I read through the next few pages, taking a fragment here and fragment there until first one story and then another came together. I went back and forth to Sigfried, who painstakingly wrote out each piece.

After hours and hours of work we were finished. The more of the stories we got written, the more the troubadours remembered until, by the end, Sigfried's makeshift stylus was nearly flying across the cloth.

"I would never have believed I could write so quickly. If only the armarius could see this!" he exclaimed. "There may be a few misspelled words or missing commas, but I think the sense comes through."

When the pitch had dried Sigfried carefully bundled the sheets of writing together and tied them securely with strips torn from the last of the tunics. I crawled back into his hood, exhausted from my reading and reciting, but feeling very triumphant. Now, all we had to do was get past the sleeping dragon.

Sigfried listened carefully to the distant snores. They were long and regular, and everyone agreed the dragon must be in a sound sleep.

"Sound as a drum," said Chaucer.

"Sound as in a body of water," said Goliard.

"Sound as in noisy," said Columba.

They went on like this for some time while Sigfried hoisted his bundle on his back. Groaning under the heaviness of his responsibility, he turned one last time to the troubadours. "The armarius was always telling me to weigh my words. Now I can see the need!" He bid farewell to the unfortunate captives, and we began the arduous climb back up through the dark caverns.

Several times, Sigfried had to stop and rest. Carrying the weight of all those stories was a heavy burden, but one he bore bravely. We groped our way back through the dark cave until we could see the coiled end of the dragon's tail in the sickly glow from his nostrils.

Suddenly, the dragon began to move and his rustling echoed menacingly through the cavern.

CHAPTER 14

Being the Undisputed Proof of Sigfried's Incredible Courage

WE SLUNK BACK AGAINST THE WALL, TRYING TO melt into the shadows. The dragon's burning gaze swept above us and we shuddered trying to keep our eyes away from his. Then Censor's great head stopped, and we could feel the heat of his stare.

"Who goes there? You are mortal, for I can smell you. But you are not one of the troubadours I have captured." He belched puffs of poisonous smoke with each word.

We cowered beneath the dragon's sneering gaze and pinched shut our noses.

"No, I . . . I . . . I am a . . . oh . . . a . . . a whoozit," Sigfried stammered.

"I have never heard of such a thing. And what is the purpose of your intrusion into my lair?"

"I . . . I . . . oh, why do words always escape me when I need them most? In any case, I have come here thinking that maybe . . . well, perhaps to see if there was any possibility . . . that is to say, it was my original intention to . . ."

This was terrible. Ever since Sigfried had

defeated the giant he seemed to have overcome his problem with words. And now it was back, worse than ever!

I leaned up and whispered in Sigfried's ear. "You had better put more conviction in your words."

"All right then," Sigfried said. "I am convinced that I might have thought . . ."

"Don't babble so," I whispered urgently in his ear. "Remember, you are the master of words now! You are the one who deciphered the note and filled in all that was missing. You are the one who unraveled the townspeople's tangle-talk. You are the one who struck a hole in the giant's overinflated vocabulary. And you are the one who has written down all of the dragon-slaying stories. We need only slip them past Censor and they will be saved."

"You are right," he said, standing tall. "I am a word master, a wordsmith." And his voice was filled with a new courage.

"Well, whoever you are," snarled the dragon, "you are not a wordy opponent for me!"

"Ah, but I am not an opponent, your malevolence," Sigfried said. "Oh no. You ask why I am here? It is to see the greatest and most magnificent rampallian in the land."

"Oh yes?" asked the dragon, seeming pleased. I guessed right away what Sigfried was doing. He was borrowing all the nastiest insults we had heard from Jargon, betting the dragon would be ignorant of their meaning, but impressed by their size.

"Oh yes, you gormless belswagger. Your reputation as the most fearsome fustilug, the most complete dandiprat, the most impressive clapperdudgeon has brought me here. I only wanted to see for myself if you were as magnificent a slubber-degullion as I had heard, and I can see that you are. And now I must be on my way."

The dragon was positively slobbering with pleasure over what he perceived as Sigfried's flattery. Molten spittle dribbled from his mouth and sizzled on the floor of the cave.

"Not so fast," he said. "This is good. This

is all very good. But you still have not told me who you are."

"Nice try," I whispered to Sigfried. "But he will never let us out of here alive, unless you are careful what you say now."

"I must not tell him my name, that is certain," Sigfried whispered back to me. "I remember from the stories how he will have power over me if he can learn my name. I must stall for time somehow."

"Tell him riddles," I whispered back. "Dragons love riddles and wasting the time trying to solve them."

The dragon gave out a grating hiss. "Speak, mortal! Who are you?"

"I am the wordsmith," Sigfried said. "I am he who can pound out the gaps in a half-told tale. I am he who cuts apart tangled chains of words and straightens out their meaning. I am he who uses the hot air from Jargon's bellows to forge a new tale of courage."

"You cannot stump me with your riddles. You are a troubadour, a bard, a storyteller!!!"

spat the dragon in great rage. His tail lashed the wall of the cavern and sent a shower of rock crumbling down at our feet.

"Maybe this wasn't such a good idea," I whispered. "You seem to have made him mad." But Sigfried wasn't listening. He had become transformed by talking. He was a different person, wielding words like a sword.

"No, Censor, your lorgship, I am no troubadour. I am he who can melt down stories and then retell them without sound!"

"That is not possible," Censor cried. "You are a liar, a counterfeit, and a sham!"

"Wrong again, Censor, oh great scroyle. I am a scribe!"

"A scribe? A scribe? What is a scribe?" demanded the dragon contemptuously, fire spouting from his nostrils.

"One who takes the fleeting words spoken by men and captures them, holds them down, and makes them last for all eternity."

"Enough of this nonsense!" cried the dragon. "The things you speak of cannot be done."

"But they can," Sigfried said. "And it has been done already." As he spoke he untied the bundle of stories from his back and held them up toward Censor like a shield. "These are the stories," Sigfried shouted. "These are the stories of dragon slaying that you are so afraid of. You can destroy the storytellers, but you cannot destroy the stories!"

The dragon reared back and then laughed, a hideous, blood-curdling laugh that echoed against the stones and reverberated all around the cave.

"Fool! That is cloth with strange markings, nothing more. It will be nothing for me to turn it to ashes!"

He opened up his great mouth to laugh again and then Sigfried did the most shocking thing. He threw the bundle of stories with all his might into the dragon's gaping jaw.

"You wanted to put your twisted words into the mouths of the troubadours," he cried. "But I shall force their words into your mouth instead."

The dragon sputtered and coughed as the stories got stuck in his throat. And then, from deep inside him came a horrible sound, like a battle far away.

"It is the pitch," Sigfried said over the din. "The pitch we wrote the stories with. It has caught fire and is exploding inside him."

We dove behind a boulder to watch.

The dragon doubled over writhing and coiling, roaring in gut-wrenching agony. He struggled for a few more minutes and then, with a thundering thud that shook us clear through to our bones, he fell, a mess of boiling blood and scorched scales.

CHAPTER 15

Wherein Sigfried Says and Becomes a Good Knight

IN A FEW MOMENTS WE HEARD THE SOUND of the troubadours feeling their way through the welter of smoke and slime. They stopped when they fell over the great carcass of the dragon.

"How did you get free of the chains?" Sigfried asked.

"They simply fell away when Censor was defeated," Barda said. "And we need never fear that he'll twist our words and bind us with them again."

Then everyone began talking at once, asking questions, expressing joy, trying to get the story straight. "Such bravery, such ingenuity, such is the stuff of which epics are created!" said Chaucer.

"This is truly marvelous," said Columba. "It seems that once Censor died, our stories came back to us, more vivid than ever."

Seeing that everyone was safe, Sigfried said, "Let us leave this place."

Gratefully we all made our way out of the cave. The smoky clouds were disappearing and the bright sunshine poured down on the scarred land.

"You are truly a linguist of the first order," Columba said. "Never again shall you be at a loss for words. And I shall compose a dithyramb as a tribute to your deeds here today."

When we reached the mule, Columba, Chaucer, Goliard, and Barda shook Sigfried's hand.

"Now, our dear friend, where will you go on your next quest?" Barda asked.

"I do not know," Sigfried said. "I am not really a knight, not even after all this. I am just a scribe who has had a wonderful adventure. Besides, this knight business is not at all the way it is portrayed in books." He paused. "Actually I am not sure what I am going to do. One thing is certain though. I do not want to return to the monastery."

I could not believe what I was hearing. I thought I knew Sigfried so well by now. I would have understood his reluctance if the dragon had defeated him. But after his victory, he could be what he'd always dreamed of.

"May I make a suggestion?" Chaucer said. "Perhaps you could still be a knight, a knight of the plume, brandishing a stylus rather than a sword. You could travel with each of us in turn and record our stories so they would never be lost again. Surely you would experience more adventure than you could hope to have in one lifetime."

"What a splendid idea!" Sigfried said. "At last, I think I have found a way with words that will suit me."

"Let us be going then," Chaucer said.

"You go ahead. I will catch up in a moment."

When we were alone, Sigfried reached up into his hood and lifted me down, setting me on a large boulder.

"I am afraid this is where we must part," he said. "You have been a good friend, but this is as far as my story goes. In this book at least.

But any time you wish to visit, you need only open the book to the beginning and our adventure will start anew. Although it will seem a slightly different story each time you read it."

And then I was at the beginning of the end, and then,

I was there. With that I closed the cover.

CHAPTER 16

Of a Deadly Game of Cat and Mouse

CLOSING THE BOOK WAS LIKE STEPPING THROUGH a door and having it slam shut behind me. My heart was still beating fast from all the excitement, and I suddenly felt very alone without Sigfried. As I tried to recall his face, my surroundings began to take shape: the dusty bookshelf on which I sat, the straight columns of books rising up in front of me, the dark void at the edge behind me. I didn't want Sigfried's story to end, and I especially didn't want to be back in the bookstore.

I stood up and stretched my tail, trying to get all the kinks out. In spite of my adventures, I was as stiff as if I had been sitting in one place.

A snuffling sound from the end of the bookshelf made it clear that the cat was still waiting for me and that there would be no escape as long as he was there.

This is silly, I told myself. Why should I be afraid of a cat when I have just faced down a dragon? The cat was a paltry thing compared to Censor. But fighting a dragon from the safety of Sigfried's hood was a very different thing than facing a cat all alone.

Still, my stomach's rumbling complaints reminded me of my cookbook. The thought of having to scrounge whatever edible words I could from the books around me didn't appeal much to my gourmet taste. There had to be some way around that blasted cat.

Making my way to the end of the shelf, I

eased myself around the last book. Two enormous hungry eyes peered up. When the cat spotted me, it leaped up, claws and fangs flashing, but it could not reach me. Still, the sight of him sent me into a cataplexy.

When I had recovered my senses, I inched behind the books, slumping down. I could hardly use any of my old tactics. Thinking about those big, empty words I had hurled down at the cat before, I realized what an onomatomaniac I had been. But more than that, reading Sigfried's story had made me very different from the meek mouse who had hidden behind a flimsy **WALL OF WORDS**. All I needed was a plan.

Perhaps I could sneak down the length of the shelf and out the other end. By the time the cat figured it out, I would be back in my haven, enjoying a succulent meal.

I began to creep along the shelf, crawling over Sigfried's book. Just standing on its beautiful embossed cover gave me the courage to go on. I scurried down the other side, trying hard not to sneeze in the dust cloud I was stirring up. With my tail over my nose I reached the end of the shelf and looked for a way down.

But my plan was a catastrophe. There stood the cat at the base of the shelf, looking up at me. I had not outwitted him at all.

"Ah, so there you are," he said. "I have been waiting for you. What have you been doing back there?"

At first I could not find my tongue, but then I realized that so long as the cat was talking, he could not be eating. So I decided to try to keep the conversation going.

"I have just been reading," I said as casually as I could in my shaky voice.

"Reading? What is reading?"

"What is reading?" I could not believe my ears. "You mean you don't know how to read?" The full extent of my past foolishness hit me then. If the cat could not read, then not only were the words that I had thrown at him meaningless, but my **WALL OF WORDS** was nothing more than scraps of paper.

"If I could read, would I ask what it is?"

My mind jumped back to the problem at hand. "Reading. Well, reading is . . ." I tried to remember what my dictionary said. "Reading is to take in the sense of letters or symbols." But after my experience with Sigfried, I knew that wasn't it at all. "It's really much more than that. A page of print is like a secret passage that leads you to worlds so far away, you cannot imagine them until the magic of reading carries you there."

The cat looked confused.

"Let me try to explain. While I was back here I opened a dusty old book that had fallen down behind the others on the shelf. And as I began to read the words, it was as if they lifted me up and carried me away to a place called medieval England." Then I told him all of Sigfried's story and the adventures we had shared. It took a long time in the telling.

When at last I had finished, the cat sighed with delight. "What a story," he cried. "What an adventure! Do you think you could teach me this thing . . . this reading?"

"I would be happy to . . ." I began to say, but then I caught the evil gleam in the cat's eye.

"If you did, I could go on these adventures myself," he said slyly. "And you . . ." He licked his chops.

And me? He would not need me. Reading was the one power that I alone possessed. If I taught it to the cat, I would be giving up my advantage.

"As I started to say, I would be happy to, but it is something only certain, very clever mice can do. I would be happy to share the *stories* I read with you. That is, if you would promise, categorically, to let me run free through the bookstore."

"You're sure you can't teach me?"

"Quite sure," I said.

"Well then, I guess I have no choice. I don't suppose *one* mouse in the bookstore will matter. It's a deal," he said. "Your stories are the only tales I want from you."

I swished my own tail with relief. Like

Sigfried, I, too had found a way with words that suited me. Promising the cat I would return soon with more stories, I scurried off to my haven and a scrumptious meal of *boeuf bourguignon*. That's French, and I wasn't sure what it was, but I was feeling very adventurous.

EPILOGUE

Of That Which Happened Thereafter

On the corner of Ninth and Market streets downtown, there is still a bookstore. And if you look in the window of that bookstore you will see long, dusty rows of faded old books. But you will not see the tip of a furry tail by *The Complete Works of Bulwer-Lytton* because Milo, the bookstore cat, no longer spends his days napping.

Some days, when Cervantes has been reading mysteries, Milo can be found sneaking around the shelves, looking for clues and pretending he is a great detective. And some days, when Cervantes has been reading Westerns, Milo can be found practicing his quick draw over by the hunting section. But some days—and these are Milo's favorites—when Cervantes has been reading fairy tales and myths, Milo can be found pretending he is a unicorn or a griffin or some other magical beast.

Cervantes no longer lives behind the reference section. When he is not reading new stories, he can be found in the cookbook section, trying out exotic new foods. He no longer cowers in fear behind a **WALL OF WORDS**, but he still insists reading is a skill that can only be mastered by mice.

And Milo—that foolish cat—believes him.